D1206350

Janosch

THE MAGIC AUTO

CROWN PUBLISHERS, INC. · NEW YORK

© 1969 Verlag Heinrich Ellermann KG, Munich, Germany. Translation © 1971 by Crown Publishers, Inc. All rights reserved. No part of this publication may be reproduced, stored in a retrieval system, or transmitted, in any form or by any means, electronic, mechanical, photocopying, recording, or otherwise, without the prior written permission of the Publisher. Inquiries should be addressed to Crown Publishers, Inc., 419 Park Avenue South, New York, N.Y. 10016. Printed in the United States of America. Library of Congress Catalog Card Number: 73-167758. **ISBN: 0-517-503174 — ISBN: 0-517-503182.** Published simultaneously in Canada by General Publishing Company Limited. **Second Printing, December, 1972**

Wasti was going to have a birthday. He would be seven years old. He felt very old and very big. But to Grandmother and Grandfather, Wasti was still their little boy, who lived with them in their neat little house.

For his birthday Wasti knew exactly what he wanted.
"An auto," Wasti said to his grandparents, "would be
the best present in the world."
But where would Grandfather get an auto?

Wasti's birthday was a bright and shining holiday for all of them. Grandfather dressed in his best clothes, and Grandmother did not work in the garden. There was a chocolate cake with seven candles. And there was an auto! Grandfather had carved it from wood, and painted it red, and the wheels could turn. It had a horn and lights. But it was very small, so small that Wasti almost cried.

"Never mind," said Grandmother. "Just you wait and see what happens. This is a magic auto."

Nothing at all happened until one
rainy day. The whole world seemed made
of water. "Maybe my auto can float
because it's made of wood," Wasti said.
"Then it would be a boat, as well."
And just then his auto began to get
bigger and bigger and bigger. It grew
like a flower in the rain, only much
faster. It grew this way and that way and
every which way until it was two
yards long. And it kept growing
until it was as large as the real
auto he had wished for.

Wasti got into his magic auto,
found the starter, stepped on the
gas, and rode away into the wide,
wide world.

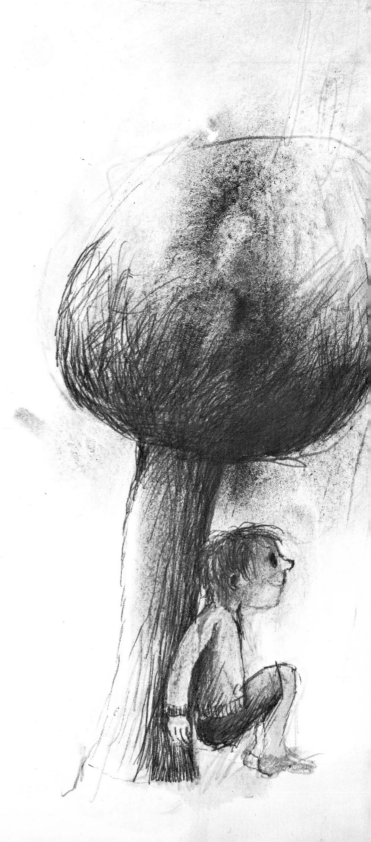

Faster and faster he drove until he was ahead of everybody
on the highway.

He even passed a racing car. The driver was very angry,
but Wasti didn't care.

Then he passed a plane. And then he passed a bird.

But the bird was flying in the other direction.

It stopped raining and Wasti thought, "What if my magic auto needs the rain to make it magic? What if it shrinks?"

But it didn't. It just went on the same as ever, zooming down the highway until they came to a big city.

Driving was much harder now. There were traffic
lights and bicyclists, and pedestrians, and policemen, and even
a skyscraper was in the way. So Wasti stepped on the gas
and drove right up the wall of the skyscraper, across
the roof, and down the other side.

"I know where we must go," Wasti said. "There's only
one place for an auto that can do such marvelous things.
We will perform at the circus!"

Wasti had never been able to afford the circus before. Today he simply drove right through the entrance and into the ring. There was a wire set up for the tightrope performers. And Wasti decided to use it.

Everyone was astonished except the elephants, who were never surprised by anything. After Wasti's daring performance he drove away fast, and he found

himself and his auto in a dark, forbidding street. In
the middle of it, a gang of robbers were getting ready for
their next holdup. It was very frightening, but the magic
auto leaped forward, the motor roared, the exhaust pipe
let out a black cloud, and the robbers ran
off in all directions.

Wasti drove on and on,
through highways and fields, wherever he
wanted to go, until he came to
a forest. And now another strange
thing happened. The auto
wound its way through the
trees just like a snake!

The birds and animals and forest people scattered
in all directions.

Once out of the forest, Wasti and his auto drove down the highway until they came to the ocean. Wasti had never seen the ocean before, and he could not see where the water ended. But they rode right in, and his auto suddenly grew smokestacks and steamed ahead like a ship.

"I could go around the world," thought Wasti to himself. "I could see Africa and India, and all the countries in my atlas, if I wanted to. But I think I won't this time."

Because, you see, Wasti was getting very hungry, and all he could think about was Grandmother's potato pancakes. So he turned around and drove over land and through water and took shortcuts through the fields until finally he came to Grandfather standing in front of the house, where it was still raining.

The rain stopped as Wasti got out of his auto, and he watched it get smaller and smaller and smaller until it was his toy auto again. He tucked it under his jacket and went inside to supper.

That evening he told Grandmother all about his trip.

"It *is* a magic auto," he said.

"Of course," said Grandmother. "An auto carved by loving hands for a boy's seventh birthday would have to be magic."

"Of course," said Wasti.